Penguin

This book is for David, with love

First edition for the United States
published in 1988 by Barron's
Educational Series, Inc.

Copyright © Susie Jenkin-Pearce 1988

First published 1988 by
Hutchinson Children's Books
An imprint of Century Hutchinson Ltd
London, England

All inquiries should be addressed to:
Barron's Educational Series, Inc.
250 Wireless Boulevard
Hauppauge, New York 11788

International Standard Book No. 0-8120-4129-1

Library of Congress Catalog Card No. 88-14649

Library of Congress Cataloging-in-Publication Data
Jenkin-Pearce, Susie.
   Peppi and Poppy search for Santa / Susie Jenkin-Pearce. — Ist ed.
for the United States.
      p.   cm.
      Summary: Peppi, a penguin who is unhappy at the zoo, accompanies a
toy penguin on his trip to visit Santa Claus and the two find a real
home at the South Pole.
      ISBN 0-8120-4129-1
      [1. Penguins—Fiction.   2. Antarctic regions—Fiction.   3. Santa
Claus—Fiction.]   I. Title.
PZ7.J412Pe 1988
[E]—dc19   88-14649

PRINTED IN ITALY
901 987654321

Peppi and Poppy
Search for Santa

Susie Jenkin-Pearce

CHILDRENS PRESS CHOICE
A Barron's title selected for educational distribution

ISBN 0-516-08697-9

Peppi was a penguin and he lived at the zoo.
   He hated his concrete home. He hated the way people leaned over the rails and stared at him. He hated fighting for food at mealtimes.

One morning, Peppi looked around him. A penguin's life is not a happy one, he thought, and he stretched his wings and sighed.

It was time for a change.

That afternoon a careless little boy dropped something into Peppi's enclosure.

Down,

down,

down

it fell.

It had an orange beak and a black coat and plippy ploppy feet, just like a penguin. But it wasn't quite the same.

"My name is Poppy and I'm a toy," she said. "And one that is not loved, for my owner has wandered off and forgotten me already."

"I'll be your friend, and I'll love you," said Peppi. And from that moment, the two were never far apart.

One day Poppy told Peppi about Santa Claus, who had given her to the little boy. "He lives at the North Pole," she said. "There are reindeer and polar bears there."

"The sea is frosty cold and the whole land is covered in ice and snow. I'd love to see Santa again. Perhaps then he would give me to someone who really loved me."

When Peppi thought of the land of ice and snow, his feathers
began to tingle. Suddenly, he knew that was where he
belonged.

"Let's fly to the North Pole!" he cried. "If you want to see
Santa Claus again, you shall."

It was a dangerous but exciting plan.

All morning Peppi did
exercises to strengthen
his wings.

Peppi borrowed some extra feathers from a seagull and Poppy
tied them to his wings.

When he was ready, he climbed to the
top of the penguin slide and leaped
off. Whoops! It was no use.
He had forgotten that penguins
can't fly.

They decided to hide in the zoo keeper's fish bucket.
  "When it is taken back to the sea," said Poppy, "we can jump
out and stow away on a ship."

So, after the next feeding time, the two friends hid in the keeper's empty bucket. Soon they were rattling along in the back of a big truck. The journey lasted a day and a night. When the truck finally stopped, the driver was astonished to see two small penguins leap out and run away.

"Which ship for the North
Pole?" cried Poppy.
   "Over there," replied
a passing seagull.

Poppy and Peppi were soon
aboard and on their way
across the ocean.

After three stormy days and nights at sea, Poppy noticed that the air was turning colder. Peppi looked through a porthole — there were lumps of ice floating on the sea.

"We're here!" he cried.

Poppy climbed on to Peppi's back and clung on tightly while he bravely leaped from the porthole. Nothing could stop them now. The two friends swam ashore.

"I'll have to go," said Poppy, tearfully, and her little beak quivered. "I must catch Santa before he sets off for Christmas Eve."

"Goodbye, and good luck," said Peppi, sadly. "I'll miss you." Peppi wandered off. He loved the feeling of the smooth cold snow in his toes and the cool fresh air under his wings.

Very soon he met some polar bears. "Good afternoon, friends,"
he said, politely. "Can you tell me where the penguins live?"

"PENGUINS! PENGUINS!" cried the polar bears in their loud
deep voices. "What are penguins?"

"I'm a penguin," said Peppi, proudly.

The bears looked him up and down. "We've never seen
anything like *you* before," they said.

Peppi began to cry. "But I know that penguins live in the land of ice and snow," he moaned.

The polar bears just laughed at him and wandered off into the white mist.

Now Peppi felt very lost and alone. Hours passed. Peppi
could see nothing but the great white world that stretched on
forever.
All of a sudden, he thought he could hear a sound — a lovely
jingly sound like little bells.

And there, through the mist, came Santa Claus on his
sleigh. And, best of all, Poppy was sitting beside him, waving.
Santa gently lifted Peppi aboard his sleigh.

"You are right — penguins do come from the land of ice and snow,"
he said. "But they live at the *South* Pole, not the *North* Pole!
I'll take you there."

Santa drove his reindeer across the wintry sky, over
the sea and far away. As they flew over the zoo, Peppi could see
all of his old friends. "They will never know the frosty
sea and feel the cold, smooth snow under their toes," he said,
sadly. "If *only* they could come too."

"And so they will," replied Santa. For on
Christmas Eve he can make wishes come true.

Santa flew his sleigh into the zoo and every penguin,
from the biggest to the smallest, climbed aboard.
And off into the sky and across the world they flew to the
South Pole.

All the penguins of the South Pole had gathered to welcome them, as if they knew they were coming.

"Here is your real home," said Santa Claus.

He gave each penguin a special present. "And this is your real home too," he said to Poppy, "for I think you *have* found someone who really loves you."

And he was gone.